NEVER TAKE A **SHARK** TO THE DENTIST

(and other things not to do)

NEVER TAKE A SHARK TO THE DENTIST

(and other things not to do)

by **JUDI BARRETT** with art by **JOHN NICKLE**

Atheneum Books for Young Readers   New York London Toronto Sydney

Never take a shark to the dentist.

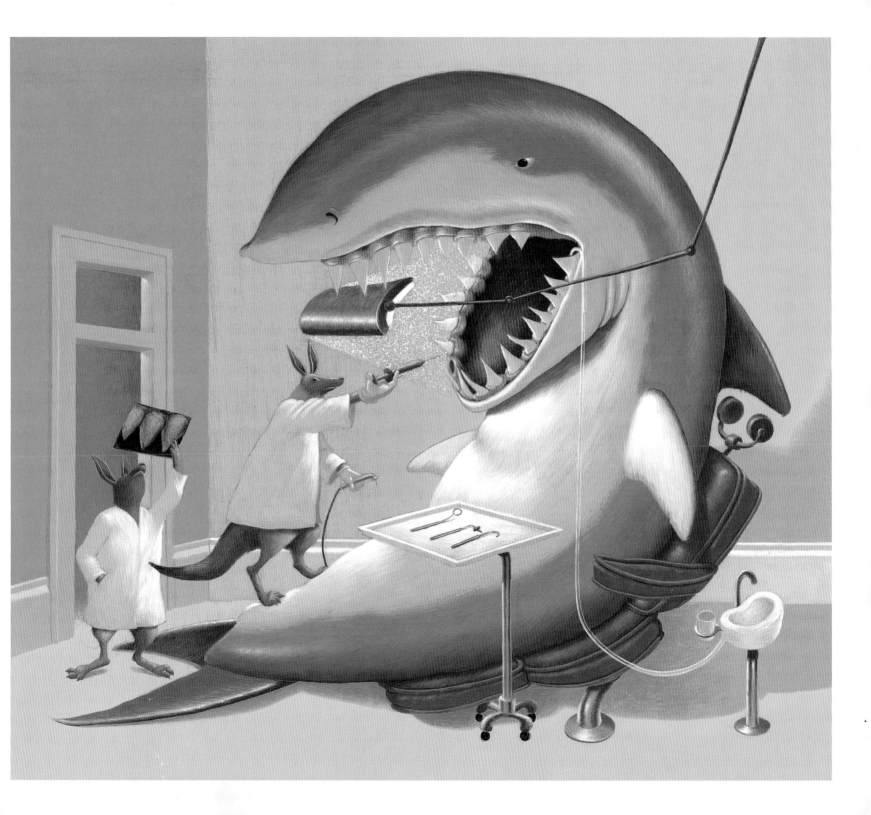

Never sit next to a porcupine on the subway.

Never go shopping for shoes with a centipede.

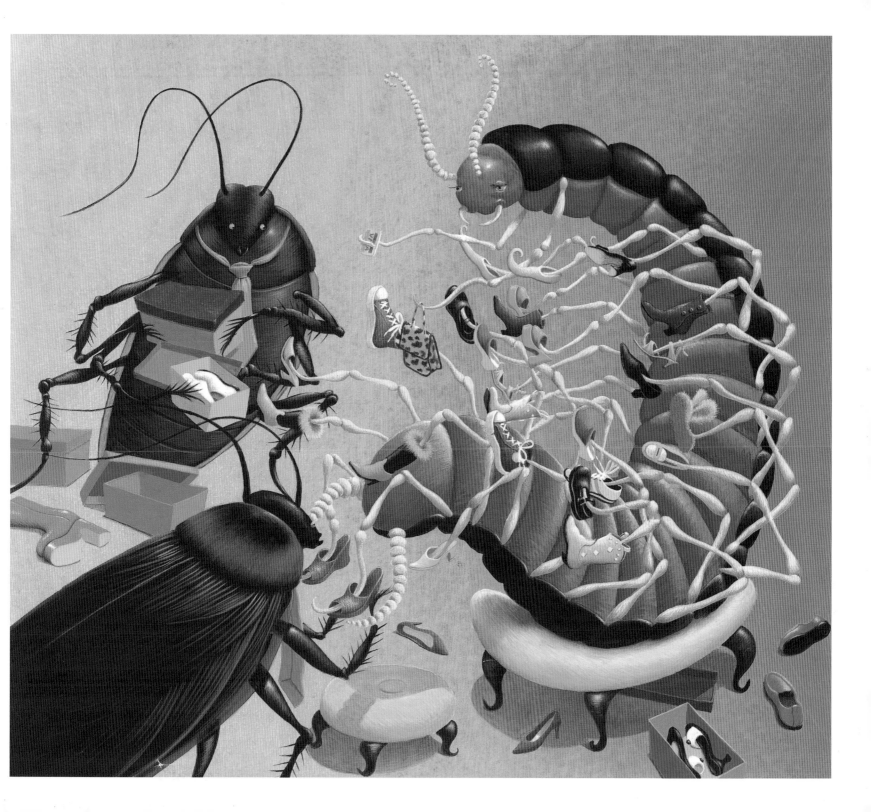

Never knit a hat for a moose.

Never invite an ant to a picnic.

Never take a giraffe to the movies.

Never play checkers with a spider.

Never share your lunch with a pig.

Never play double Dutch with a grasshopper.

Never hold hands with a lobster.

Never take a goat with you to the library.

Never give a moth a sweater for her birthday.

Never go to the bank with a raccoon.

But *always* go shopping with a pelican.

To Sasha —J. B.

To Brianna —J. N.

Atheneum Books for Young Readers • An imprint of Simon & Schuster Children's Publishing Division •
1230 Avenue of the Americas • New York, New York 10020 • Text copyright © 2008 by Judi Barrett •
Illustrations copyright © 2008 by John Nickle • All rights reserved, including the right of reproduction in
whole or in part in any form. • Book design by Michael McCartney • The text for this book is set in Matrix
and Matrix Script. • The illustrations for this book were rendered in acrylic paint. • Manufactured in China •
• 10 9 8 • Library of Congress Cataloging-in-Publication Data • Barrett, Judi • 1013 SCP
Never take a shark to the dentist and other things not to do / Judi Barrett ; illustrated by John Nickle.—
1st. ed. • p. cm. • Summary: A list of things one should not do with various animals, such as "hold hands
with a lobster." • ISBN-13: 978-1-4169-0724-4 • ISBN-10: 1-4169-0724-6 • [1. Animals—Fiction.] I. Nickle,
John, ill. II. Title. • PZ7.B2752Nev 2007 • [E]—dc22 2006000153